ICE TO DUST

Amaya Sego

Brass Ink Publishing

CONTENTS

Prologue

The snow was magical as it fell from the sky. The first few days were beautiful. Then, the big freeze happened. The beautiful snowy landscape turned to solid ice. No one had ever seen temperatures drop this low in the United States since 1899. Though it was only for three weeks, it created a catastrophic domino effect. Heating units gave out. Waterlines froze and burst. Even electronics inside of buildings didn't come out unscathed. All of the liquid in vehicles froze, damaging engines. Once a plane landed, the engine would seize leaving it grounded. Most animal and insect life froze leaving the earth quiet. The few people that survived did so either by hunkering down in an underground shelter or through sheer miracle. Life as we knew it was over. In the beginning, the few people in each town banded together. Loved ones were buried in backyards since there was no one to run the mortuary. The occasional arsonist could get a crematorium up and running for those who didn't have land to bury on.

After the initial shock had worn off and emotions raged, people were out for themselves. Sometimes they stayed in small groups, sometimes people opted to become loners. After a couple of years, a new enemy arose. Criminals had banded together, scouring the area for people. They became slave traders, feared by all. If you weren't scrounging for food and supplies, you were hiding, or running for your life. Some days, all of the above. America had become a wasteland.

CHAPTER 1

The distance to my camp was a little over a hundred yards. Not a tough walk. I had done it hundreds of times. The problem today was that I had to run it. The ragged, burlap potato sack that hung from a carabiner on my green harness held a couple of cans of beans and a can of vegetable soup. A blessing and a curse. I had snagged it from my stash in an abandoned grocery store, which meant I would eat tonight and tomorrow morning. That's if my five-foot four-inch, 130-pound frame could make it to my camp at a dead run with the extra weight.

Two days ago, a new group of wastelanders set up camp in the open, desolate space. They had no protective perimeter to speak of. That meant they were either stupid or dangerous. Of which, I didn't want to find out. Three faded green makeshift canvas tents were set up. A beastly cargo truck was parked behind them. Behind the cab of the vehicle was a modified enclosed structure big enough for several people to stand in. From where I stood, I could hear a generator running. I was glad they hadn't encroached on my area.

I waited in the abandoned grocery store until

nightfall. I decided I'd walk as long as I could and break into a run if I was spotted. I took ten steps into the open area and the generator shut off. Silence.

Fuck! If they cut me off, a vulture's breakfast would be my end. After an extended day of exploring, I was too tired to head back and make the three-mile trek through the hills to avoid the open, now-inhabited space. I walked as light footed as I could over the ivory dusted gravel. In the full moonlight, I'd be easy to spot. Even though I had walked the train tracks to the next town, my ragged black, long-sleeved shirt, and my burgundy pants were covered in dust. If I made it to my camp, I'd probably be able to see the outline where my faded green harness sat.

As I walked calmly, I pulled my back pocket-length, almond-colored braid over my shoulder and tucked it under my gray scarf. It made me stand out, yet I still refused to cut it. Thankfully, I had the luxury of a brush.

Even though I had resolved myself to death, my heart still pounded as I walked. I cleared the end of the vehicle and sucked in a deep breath. I hadn't realized I'd been holding it. I relaxed my steps but then made the careless, dire mistake of kicking a rock. The noise echoed around me.

"Intruder!" I heard a male voice yell from the camp.

"Fuck!" I said out loud. I broke into a run. I reached down and grabbed the neck of the burlap sack to keep it from banging against my leg. The wind blew my scarf off my head. I glanced back. Two men and a woman were chasing me. Their boots pounded the rocky ground behind me.

Adrenaline flowed more freely than before. I was surprised to clear the dead tree line a short way up the hill. My territory. I could navigate this area with my eyes closed. I slid into a deep divot in the ground that was covered in leaves and branches, instantly disappearing. I took slow deep breaths and waited.

The three people cleared the tree line, evidenced by the crunching on dead, dry leaves. "Spread out!" yelled a man with a voice like thunder. Their footsteps seemed to go in different directions. One set walked so close to my hiding place that I thought he would trip over the frame that the branches were attached to.

At least one set of footsteps faded up the hill. *Dammit!* I would have to wait here until they gave up! Not something wastelanders do very often. I strained my ears to listen past my pounding heart. The familiar scent of earth filled my nostrils, but there was something else there too. I breathed in deeply. Another whiff. It was pleasant but I couldn't identify it.

"He disappeared, Lucas!" I heard a man yell as a set of footsteps descended the hill. It was a slightly higher pitched voice than the one that told them to spread out.

"I don't think it's a 'he'," boomed the low voice once again. It startled me because it was so close.

"He or she, there's only one," said a female voice coming from the direction of my camp.

Fuck! They had found it. My sanctuary.

I lay in the darkness for a while after the footsteps faded down the hill. My stomach rumbled, telling me it was time to get up. As stealthy as I could, I slipped from my hiding spot, heading back to my camp. I made a fire under a grate that sat across two stacks of red bricks. The vegetable soup revived me after a day of exploring, running, and hiding. I'd hoped that it, coupled with the cooler night of fall, would help me sleep.

CHAPTER 2

I got up out of bed for what seemed like the hundredth time to peek out of the dusty fabric that covered my hole in the hill. The sky was lighter, but the sun hadn't cleared the hill peak opposite mine.

A cold can of beans wasn't nearly as satisfying as the hot vegetable soup, but it filled the empty spot in my stomach. I strapped on my harness, this time attaching two rusty machetes in their sheaths crossed on my back. I'd found them both in an old, leaky shed. If I didn't kill someone with them, tetanus would finish the job.

I crept to the tree line and crouched behind a tree. No movement around the camp and no generator running yet. The distance between me and the desolate town used to be a minor annoyance. Now, as I stepped out into the open, it felt like a life-or-death risk. All before a full day of scouting.

I made if further than I had last night before anyone saw me.

"Lucas!" cried a woman's voice this time. "She's out of hiding!"

I broke into a run. I guess as a woman,

she would recognize another woman, even from a distance and with my scarf covering my head.

My lungs and legs were both burning like fire by the time I reached my hiding place in the abandoned grocery store. The familiar musty smell of wood that had been rained on hit my nose as I stepped through the door. I rushed in and peered through a broken window in the back of the building. A wild hailstorm a couple of years ago had shattered several windowpanes.

No one from the new camp had followed me. I leaned against the wall and slid down to the hardwood floor to finish catching my breath. My annoyance grew to anger. Now I had two enemies to avoid, on top of trying to survive daily life. *Dammit!*

The days were shorter now that it was fall, so I pushed myself off of the floor to get crackin'. As I got up, the sound of a beastly truck in the distance caught my ear. But the direction was wrong. I peered out of the broken window again. Still nothing.

The sight I caught through the door of the front of the building was far worse than nothing. Three enormous trucks with giant metal cages on the back were rumbling in my direction. *Fuck!*

I had avoided becoming a slave each month since the big freeze four years ago. I'd be damned if it happened today. The trucks slowed to let soldiers out. Each building in this square would be thoroughly searched before they moved on. I closed the door to give me a bit more time and a noise warning.

The thick chunky soles of my leather boots served me well as I dashed to the back of the building and kicked out the rest of a set of windows. Perched on the windowsill, I turned around and stood up. The short peek design in the metal roofing gave me something to cling to. The decrepit white paint crumbled under my boots as I fought to climb up. Thankfully the front facade of this building was a rectangle that didn't follow the pitch of the roof. The rumble of the slave trucks grew nearer. I crawled across the roof, hoping I wouldn't fall through. When I made it to the front of the building, I glanced over the short wall. Seven to ten soldiers were going in and out of buildings as the trucks slowly drove through the square. Their stolen, but dusty blue, uniforms that they wore, coupled with the plasma guns that they carried, made for a menacing sight. The sun had hardly crested the hills and there were already people in one of the cages.

Dammit! Those poor people. Life was enough of a struggle if you were free.

I stayed crouched down out of view. The two machetes on my back wouldn't save me today, but hiding? That I could do. As they got closer, I could hear the soldiers yelling over the noise of the engines that the buildings were clear. The vibration of the men opening and slamming the door of the building I was on made me tremble with fear. The surge of adrenaline raced through me like a flash of heat.

Satisfied with clearing the rest of the town

square, they moved on...right toward the new wastelanders' camp.

I dared not turn to look. I only listened. About a minute later, there was a sound like a crack of thunder. It was so loud that it made my ears ring. The deafening sound was followed by the swift acceleration of the slave trucks. They flew past me in quick succession. It didn't take long for the rumble of the slave trucks to vanish completely.

Fuuuuuck! The people in the new camp were more dangerous than I thought. And I still had to pass them with whatever I found today to get back to my sanctuary.

I slid off the roof and hit the ground with a roll. My destination? One town over. I kept an eye out for people the closer I got to the deserted town.

In the beginning I had spent weeks stashing supplies, canned food, and tools. Stores, factories, and other businesses looked like they had been picked clean, hence the reason people moved on. Selfish, I know. Stashing everything in my camp meant that I would lose everything if the slave patrols ever ventured past the dead tree line and found it again. I couldn't haul a vast amount in a vehicle because it would be too conspicuous to drive in the open, especially with no place to hide it afterward. That was if I could even find a vehicle and make it run. The new wastelanders' beastly truck was the first complete vehicle I'd seen in almost a year other than the slave patrols.

The floorboards in the General Store pulled

away easily. I grabbed activated charcoal for my water filtration system and three more cans of soup. I replaced the boards and made my exit. The sun was hot and sweat poured off my face. It still felt like summer during the day even though the fall nights were cooler.

When I finally returned to my own deserted town, I went to the hardware store. Moving wall panels from the side of the store revealed the pickaxe that I needed. I'd start a new cave tomorrow...if I made it through the night.

Fall had become a fast friend. The earlier night fell, the earlier I could make it home. The thought of the extra three mile walk through the hills instead of the hundred or so yards to my camp seemed to grate me more after such a long day. Now I had a pickaxe that added to the weight that I carried.

I made it three-quarters of the way to the tree line before I heard footsteps pounding toward me. *Shit!* My heart jumped and so did I. My quads burned with soreness from the day before as I raced for the tree line. Shrouded in darkness by the trees, I flung the pickaxe to my left. I'd have to retrieve it in the morning. This time I slipped behind a large tree. It was almost pitch dark. From the one glance over my shoulder, I saw that no one carried a light source. I hoped that their eyes weren't as accustomed to seeing in the dark as I was.

I heard the crunching of dead leaves. They'd cleared the tree line.

"It's like she slipped into another dimension," said the female voice.

The group didn't do much searching, but I waited several long minutes after they'd gone to move. Cold soup is gonna suck but, I can't risk a fire to heat it. I suddenly despised them even more.

CHAPTER 3

The next several days held more of the same. In the mornings, just after dawn, I made my way safely into town. In the evenings, I was running for my life. Each day I would alternate between camouflaged divots in the ground and the thick trunk of a tree.

I opted for that three mile walk back this afternoon. It crossed a river too. The water wasn't clean enough to drink, but a swim would serve as both a bath and doing laundry in one.

The chilly water invigorated me as it washed off the stench of dried sweat. Once I began to shiver, I climbed out.

Back in my covered shallow cave, I tossed my dry harness with the machetes over a wooden chair, the pickaxe leaning next to it. I was about to peel my wet, long-sleeved shirt off when I heard the crack of a dead branch. I froze. *Fuck!* Not many animals still lived in this dusty forest. I moved the fabric of my dwelling just enough to see. In the dim light of dusk, I saw a large figure creeping toward me. I tore back the fabric and bolted. The dark figure thundered in my direction. It was hard to run in my unlaced boots. I'd made it maybe twenty yards when the right one came off. On the next bare-footed step I dashed my toes against a jagged rock. Pain exploded through my foot. As I tumbled to the ground, the other boot flew off. "Fuck!" I yelled as a rolled a few times. I tried to get up but stepped on a sharp twig.

I glanced behind me just as this giant of a man reached me. He wrapped his massive hand around my upper left arm, keeping me from falling again. I tried to swing but he caught my fist.

"Are you hurt?" His voice rumbled through my chest. Lucus. This was who the deep voice from last night belonged to.

"Fuck! Yes, you were chasing me, asshat! Wait, why do you care?" My chest heaved and my foot throbbed with pain.

"Just being cautious. Clearly you aren't a threat. Now, are you hurt?" he asked, this time his deep voice softened. I was annoyed at his comment, but he was still holding me up as I balanced on my left foot.

"Yes," I looked down at my foot and saw blood on my first two toes. He moved his hand from my fist to my forearm. I instinctively grabbed his. Solid as a rock. I'd have no chance fighting him off if I wanted to. "I need my boots to walk back," I said, glancing around.

He crouched down and swooped me up like a baby.

"Wait! No! I'm still wet!" I hollered, suddenly caring for his well-being.

While holding me in his arms, he effortlessly

squatted down and picked up both of my boots.

"Why are you helping me? Other than the fact that you just chased me down?" I asked expecting the question to get me dropped on my ass.

"Contrary to most wastelanders' beliefs, allies can be a good thing," he replied, his deep voice rumbling through me even more deeply. I needed to get my mental shit together!

I started to lean up as we approached my cave, but he tightened his grip.

"Wait, my camp is that way," I said in a sudden panic, pointing in the direction of my dwelling.

"We have medical supplies and warm water to clean your wounds," Lucas said, soothingly. "It's the least I can do for causing you to fall."

Emotions conflicted within me. On one hand, I had gone from being completely independent to being carried because I was injured. On the other, someone cared enough to carry me.

We were about ten yards from the camp when Lucas set my feet on the ground. Not letting my upper body go, he retrieved a control box out of his dark gray pants pocket. He pushed a button and scooped me up again. After several steps forward, Lucas pushed the button again. I could feel the muscles in his arms contract as he did so. Man, I was in some serious trouble.

"What was that?" I asked.

"Invisible electric perimeter," Lucas replied, bringing the control box into view from under my bent knees. "Don't leave without letting us know or you'll get fried."

"Noted," I replied. Shit! Dangerous, not stupid. And now I was trapped.

A woman with long brown and red dread locks met us at their beastly truck. "What happened?" she asked in alarm.

"This is what happens when you don't tie your boots," Lucas said in jest.

She smacked him in the arm. "Just in case you can't tell, this is my step-sister, Pyka," he said.

"I'm Charlie," I replied. Lucas raised an eyebrow in question. "Charlotte is the whole thing, but I prefer Charlie. Wow, it's been a long time since I've said my own name." I'm sure the surprise was apparent on my face.

"Pyka, can you get her some clothes so she can shower?"

"Sure," Pyka replied brightly before she headed off towards her tent.

"Shower? I just had a bath," I said in defense. I must have looked like a giant child when I crossed my arms over my chest, but I didn't care.

You went swimming in the river," Lucas chuckled, raising both eyebrows at me.

"Same difference. And it also means I did laundry. I was about to peel my clothes off and let them dry when you decided to test my threat level by chasing me through the rocky woods." A fall breeze blew over me and I shivered.

"You need a hot shower and dry clothes,"

Lucas said in a firm but caring tone. "And I need to tend to your wounds."

My mouth dropped open, but before I could say anything Pyka had returned with dry clothes. "Don't worry, my step-brother's a doctor."

I just closed my mouth. Pyka smiled. "These are clean, I promise," she said and handed me the stack. Everything was faded, as to be expected, but they were soft and they smelled clean. All the clothes I had ever scavenged already had that dusty smell. Even that was a welcomed after wearing nothing but river washed clothes.

"Thank you," I smiled back. It might be nice to have a female friend. There were a couple of women in the group that left me almost a year ago, but we weren't very close.

"I need to set you down for just a second," Lucas said as he seated me on a short ledge on the back of the truck. He walked around to the side of the truck and yanked the cord. The generator roared to life. He came back around, picked me up, and carried me up into the back of the truck.

When the door closed, the generator was barely audible. It was like they had loaded a spacious travel trailer into the back of a diesel cargo truck. There was more than enough room to walk around. It had a shower, a toilet, a sink, and a bench to sit and dress yourself. At the end towards the cab was a bed. The lights were unusually bright. Brighter than any of the homes I'd seen before the big freeze.

In this light I could see him clearly. Setting

me back on my feet, he could have rested his chin on my head. His wavy brown hair sat just below his shoulders. The bottom half of his well-trimmed beard grazed his chest when he spoke. The span of his chest was almost two of me. Even in brief glances, his deep brown eyes penetrated my very being.

He spoke, shaking me from my thoughts. "The water won't take long to get hot," he said as he slid the shower door open.

"Thank you, I'll be quick," I replied. Clean water was more precious than jewels in this world after the big freeze.

"No need. We have a 50-gallon tank. Once the water goes down the drain, it goes back into the filtration system. It will get reheated and reused," he explained as he turned on the hot and cold water. "Take as long as you need. Pyka has shampoo in there too. I'll be right here if you need anything."

He pulled the curtain across the room that separated the bathroom area from the bed. It felt awkward undressing with him still in there. I peeled off my wet clothes as quickly as I could and tossed them into the sink. I almost lost my balance trying to stay off my wounded foot.

The hot water streamed down my cold body. I let it pour down my face as I undid my sopping wet, wind-blown braid.

The rose shampoo smelled incredible. I felt a little guilty for using so much, but unbraided and wet, my hair reached mid-thigh. It took me a while to get the shampoo worked though it all. I finally picked the soap up and began to lather. The scent hit my nose and brought me back to yesterday.

"This is what I smelled while I was in a hole the other day."

"What was?" he replied.

"This soap. I smelled it while you guys were looking for me. You were standing close enough to my hiding place that I caught a whiff of it."

"We raided a soap factory just as things were getting bad. All the extra space in here is filled with it."

The soap had finally made its way to my wounded foot. "Arg!" I hollered. "Fuck, this hurts!"

"What hurts?" asked Lucas, this time with urgency in his voice. I was suddenly afraid he would come into the shower to find out for himself.

"My foot," I answered quickly.

"I'll have a look at it when you get out," he replied, over the pouring water.

After rinsing all of the soap and shampoo off, the stinging pain in my foot subsided. The hot water was healing, but I forced myself to turn it off. A burst of cold air hit my wet skin when I slid opened the shower door. As I stepped out to grab a towel he said, "Don't get dressed yet."

Fuck! I snatched the towel off the stack that sat on the dressing bench. Shaking it open, I flung it around me and tucked in the end. My body started to shake as Lucas pushed the curtain aside. I was thankful the soft faded, gray towel stopped a few inches above my knees.

"H-how do we do this?" I stammered. All my nerve had disappeared. My eyes were glued to the floor, searching for it.

"Have a seat," he said, gesturing towards the foot of the bed. He produced a tattered black duffle bag from under the sink before grabbing a stool to sit in front of me.

I sat on the edge of the bed clutching the towel to keep it in place. Lucas took up so much space in front of me that I had nowhere to focus on but him. I opted to just squeeze my eyes shut. *Dammit*, where was my nerve when I needed it?

Lucas rested a warm, firm hand on my shoulder. "You've survived this long by hiding, haven't you, Charlie?"

"Yes," I answered quietly. He squeezed my shoulder, causing me to take a deep breath and relax.

"Let me know if anything I do hurts," he said.

He lifted my foot by the ankle. His touch was electrifying. I tried to control my breathing as my heart shifted into overdrive. My first two toes were starting to bruise. The cuts spanned the first three toes. "This is going to sting like a bitch," he said as he applied iodine to the wounds.

I sucked in a deep breath. "Fuck! Yes, accurate on that one!" Yes, there was my nerve. It had returned for only a moment when the pain was surpassed by the pressure on my calf. He was gently squeezing the muscle. His thick hand squeezed all the way up to the back of my knee. He repeated the actions on the other leg. His touch sent waves of sparks flying in all directions. Goosebumps rose with a vengeance. I could feel myself blushing hard.

Pyka stepped into the truck just in time to save me. "How are you feeling?" she asked.

"Much better now that I'm actually clean and dry," I replied.

"Would you like Pyka to stay?" asked Lucas, thoughtfully. I'm guessing he sensed my trepidation or saw how red my face was.

"Yes please," I replied.

Pyka smiled. "Absolutely, hun." She sat on the bed and held my hand to comfort me.

"Charlie, you'll have to let the towel drop a bit so I can listen to your heart and lungs," Lucas said, producing a stethoscope from the bag. "Normally I would have done this to start with, but you needed to get used to my touch first."

I took a deep breath. I could do this. Pulling the towel loose, I let it drop. I noted the warm stethoscope. He must have warmed it in his hand before touching me with it. Another sign that he cared.

"Breathe deep, Charlie," said Lucas. I complied. I'm sure he heard my heart speed up the moment his giant hand landed on my bare back. Warmth and tingling radiated in all directions. "Your heart is strong," he said after listening for several seconds.

Pyka rubbed my arm. Lucas put his hand on my shoulder when he moved to my back to listen to my lungs.

"This is the most touch I've had in months. I didn't realize how much I needed it," I said, taking a deep breath. I felt relaxed for the first time in a very long time.

"I'm glad you trust us," Pyka said. She just radiated joy and happiness without being overly hyper. I smiled at her, thankful for her company.

When it was time for the torso exam, Pyka climbed up on the bed and held both my hands. With my head on a pillow in her lap she asked, "What did you do before the big freeze?"

"I worked on big movie sets. I helped actors dress for movies. They could do most of it themselves, but some costumes were easier to put on with help. Sometimes I had to do research and hunt down a specific article of clothing for a movie. What about you, Pyka?" Guess I ramble when I'm nervous too.

"I was a radio host on an evening show. It was fun interviewing people. I really liked hearing people's stories. Working at the station was probably what saved me. A few of us stayed inside the soundproof booth. We always had snacks stashed. We just stayed huddled together and pretended to interview each other. Learned a lot those few weeks." There was a little sadness in her voice towards the end.

Lucas palpated the soft flesh of my torso. I was beginning to get used to his touch, but it was still exhilarating. I squirmed when he hit the ticklish spots on my sides. His eyes twinkled when he smiled. "What's this from?" Lucas asked, touching a small scar in my naval.

"I decided kids weren't for me in this lifetime," I replied. "Some people said I was selfish for doing it. Then the big freeze happened. People told me I was the smart one after that."

Once Lucas was satisfied I had only a few bumps and bruises he bandaged my wounded foot. By then, my shame was gone so I just got up and got dressed.

"Umm… what do I do with my wet clothes and the towel?" I asked, not wanting to be any more of a burden on anyone.

"Hang them in here," Pyka said, opening a door that I hadn't noticed before. It went from the ceiling to about my waist. I hung the towel from industrial spring clips suspended from a metal hanger. Several hangers hung on a thick rod. "High powered jets of water and soap will get them clean. In the next chamber, the air from the generator is filtered before it hits the clothes to dry them."

"It's been a long time since I've had on clothes not cleaned in the river," I said, still in shock.

"You okay sleeping in my tent tonight? We shut the generator off at night so the truck will be pitch black and hot," said Lucas as he helped me out of the back of the truck.

I was so tired of being alone, but this was a total stranger…a stranger that bandaged my wounds after allowing me a hot shower and fresh clothes. "Can I think about it?"

"Of course," Lucas replied.

The beef and pasta MRE was a great change in menu. A hot shower and a full stomach made it hard to stay awake. I leaned towards the fire and began running my fingers through my damp hair. I was mesmerized by the flames until a memory came back to me. "Here's one for you," I said, still staring into the fire. "I was in the building closest to here in town when I heard a blast yesterday. Right after that, the slave traders flew past me like a bat outta hell. What happened?"

"Our plasma gun is bigger than their plasma guns," replied Dimitri, pointing to a black spot on the ground. In the fire light, it shined like wet tar splattered across the white gravel. My eyes went wide in shock that the smudge used to be a human being.

"You shot him as he touched the electric perimeter, Dimitri. You knew what would happen," laughed Lucas.

"I was trying to make a point. And you can't over kill anyone. They are either dead or they're not. The combination simply negated the need for burial."

"And sent those slave traders fleeing for their lives, which makes me glad I'm on your side," I threw in.

"Was that a one off or a regular thing?" Lucas asked in a more serious tone.

"They come around about once a month.

They search all the buildings in town before they hit this giant cul-de-sac. Hence the reason for all my camouflaged burrows."

"Have they ever found your camp?" asked Pyka.

"Once, a few months ago. It was closer to the tree line. Had to rebuild everything," I replied.

"How do you survive out here?" Lucas asked.

"The buildings in town are filled with supplies. There are a couple of towns within a day's walking distance along the train tracks that I venture to from time to time," I replied.

Lucas tilted his head in question, "We searched all of the buildings. They're all empty except for shelves and display cases."

"That's because I made them look that way," I replied with cocky smile. Lucas arched his brow at me, so I continued. "I'm resourceful. I'll show you all my secrets tomorrow."

"Ready to get some rest then?" Lucas asked me. He stood up and held out his hand to me.

I looked at Lucas' hand like a deer in headlights. *Fuck it!* They didn't kill me, and they fed me. "Yes!" I grabbed his hand. "Good night, everyone."

"Good night," said Dimitri.

"Good night, Charlie. Thank you for the chat. We definitely need some girl time," said Pyka with a smile.

"Yes, please," I said, returning her smile.

Lucas chuckled. "Hey Dimitri, you got the fire?" he asked.

"Yeah," Dimitri replied.

Lucas pulled me into his tent. A small lantern lit the area nicely. His cot with a thin mattress looked like it could sleep two, or maybe just him comfortably. On the right side of the tent was a folding table with a giant plasma gun. It cleared the table on both ends by several inches.

"Is that what killed one of the slave traders yesterday?" I asked, stepping closer to have a look.

"Dimitri used his, but yes," said Lucas. He sat on the cot and undid his boots. They were followed by his faded blue pants.

"You sleep without pants on?" I asked in surprise.

"They won't be looking at my underwear when I come out of my tent holding that," he said, nodding towards the plasma gun. I couldn't help but stare at his muscular legs.

"I'm guessing you don't?" he said, bringing my eyes back to his face.

"I haven't slept without being fully dressed in years. I ditched my pants one unbearably hot summer night. Even though I was exhausted I couldn't hit the sleep realm. Finally put my pants back on and crashed out."

His piercing brown eyes bore into mine. "You're safe here. We are surrounded by an electric perimeter. We have several plasma guns that aren't visible. And you'll be sleeping next to me. You'll be more comfortable without pants on, but you don't have to." His voice was calm and soothing.

I took a deep breath in and let it go. Could I let my guard down for tonight? I walked around to the left side of the bed. It was deeper in the tent where the fabric sloped down. Lucas's body obscured some of the lantern light making it dimmer on this side of the bed. I sat down and took my boots off. As I stood to shed my pants, I paused. I suddenly felt vulnerable again. I heard the cot creak. It sounded like Lucas was getting under the covers. Warmth spread over me when Lucas put his hand on my thigh and squeezed gently.

"You can put your pants back on at any time. You don't have to do this if you don't want to." The genuine concern on his face floored me. Even the group I was with almost a year ago hadn't cared this much by the end of the three-ish years together.

"I can do this. I can trust you. I resolved myself to death when you guys set up camp, but you've bandaged my wounds, fed me, and jump-started the healing process after months of being alone," I told him. He gave my thigh another squeeze before laying back down. I undid my pants and slid them down. I could feel Lucas staring at the blue flowery cotton panties Pyka had given me. I folded my pants and put them on top of my boots. When I laid down, I was rigid. I positioned myself as close to the edge of the mattress as I could without falling off. I was thankful for a soft bed but didn't want to encroach on his space.

"Come here. Face me," Lucas commanded. His arm was lifted. As I rolled over and scooted closer, he wrapped his massive arm around me. I had no choice but to lay my head on his shoulder. He bent his knee, nudging it between my thighs. I gasped. "This will help keep you warm." His voice was calming.

I was only stiff for a few moments before my body started to relax. "That's if I can sleep," I replied, and then yawned. There were very few nights when I slept for more than a few hours at a time.

"Do you want me to move?" It was a question that again showed me that he cared for my well-being.

"No, it's actually very grounding," I replied. He flung the covers over both of us. Another layer of protection. It took me a few moments to realize that I had wrapped my legs around his giant one and crossed my feet at the ankles. I tried to figure out what to do with the arm that wasn't pinned between us. My fingertips grazed his beard, and I jerked my hand back.

"You can touch it," Lucas said. Laying against his side made his voice rumble through my chest.

I reached again and began stroking is beard. It was smoother than I expected it to be.

"That feels nice," he said. He was being vulnerable with me. Okay, I can do this. I wiggled trying to get just a little closer, not sure it was possible, and he tightened his arm around me. His thigh came up a fraction of an inch. He'd locked me against him. I was safe. It didn't take but a few more strokes of his beard before I crashed. Hard.

CHAPTER 4

Despite the thick canvas tent, I woke up to the sound of voices. I raised my head to find that I was alone but still cozy, wrapped in a blanket. I really didn't want to get up, but the light coming through the tiny gap in the tent told me it was well past sunrise. I had actually slept through the night. I got up and got dressed. Heading out of the tent, my nose was met with the aroma of coffee. The smell was divine. It was yet another thing that I hadn't had in longer than I could remember.

"Feel better?" Lucas asked as he poured me a cup of coffee. They had a morning fire going with a grate over it. It was heating water for more MREs next to a metal coffee percolator.

"That's the best night's sleep I've had since this became a wasteland," I replied, gratefully accepting the cup of coffee.

"You ready to show us what you do every day?" asked Dimitri over his steaming mug.

"After that night's sleep and everything yesterday, I'll take you anywhere you want to go. I'll even show you where all of my hiding places are if we have to take cover," I replied before taking a sip of coffee. It was more wonderful than I had remembered.

"Are any of those holes of big enough for Lucas?" laughed Dimitri.

"Um... he may have to climb a tree. Or we can dig a bigger hole before we even have the need make a run for it."

"I'm glad you trust us," said Pyka, coming to stand next to me with her own cup of coffee. It was a chilly, so she leaned with her arm against mine.

"I figured the alternative was death, which I would gladly take over being caught by the slave traders," I replied.

"Me too, in a heartbeat," said Pyka.

CHAPTER 5

After breakfast, we prepared to leave for town. Even though it was a short distance from camp, Lucas insisted that we all carry plasma pistols in leg holsters. They had several extra, so they gave me one too.

"The blast radius is pretty big, but these only carry ten shots, so don't miss," said Lucas as he helped me strap on the leg holster. His touch sent tingles down my leg.

"Thank you for the protection, but I feel naked without my harness. It has karabiners and my burlap sack to carry stuff," I told them.

"Dimitri, grab the smallest duffle bag we have. Today is more about scouting for us. If we bring back anything, it won't be much," said Lucas.

"The slave traders only come once a month, so hopefully we'll be safe," I said, trying to keep an even tone.

"But we shot one of their own," said Dimitri as he strapped on his own leg holster.

"Dimitri's right. They may come back sooner with reinforcements," said Lucas.

"Are we going to take the truck?" asked Pyka.

"We'll leave the electric perimeter up and walk. Their trucks are faster than ours. Unless they have a catapult, they're not getting into the camp," replied Lucas.

Once we were ready, we all stood at the edge of the perimeter. You could barely see the tip of the metal rod that had been driven into the ground. I could feel my hair starting to stand on end, which was brushed and braided thanks to Pyka. Lucas pulled out a small control box from one of his many pants pockets and disabled the perimeter. As soon as we were a few feet past it, he reenabled it.

We walked in companionable silence until we were close to town. The crunch of the rocky terrain under our boots seemed louder than usual.

"See the paint missing on the back of that wall?" I asked in a low voice. I knew it was only us but the need to stay stealthy hung heavy in the air.

"Yeah," Lucas nodded. He inclined his head towards me to hear better.

"That was from me scrambling up to the roof the day the slave traders came. I was in that building and had to kick out that window. I hid up there until they flew back past me."

"How did you get down?" asked Pyka.

"Tuck and roll," I said with a cocky grin. Finally, I had gotten a little of my spunk back.

"And there are supplies in here?" asked Dimitri. I nodded. "We checked in here, it was empty, I swear."

"Let me show you," I said as we stepped

through the door. "This used to be a grocery store." I walked up to the first wall panel and felt for the little gap. Pulling the panel free, I leaned it against the one beside it. I did that for every other panel all the way to the back of the building. "We have soup, we have veggies, a couple of cans of pie filling if you want something sweet. Probably not my best idea, but under a few of the floorboard is all the pasta. I just need a small tool to pry up the end of the board, but most of it is the same stuff that's in the walls." The rest of the group looked at the rations in awe.

"What made you think of this?" asked Pyka.

"If they busted me with it at my camp, it would all be gone. So, I hid it in plain sight. The slave traders haven't figured it out yet, so as long as I don't get caught, I get to keep eating," I replied.

"Let's check out the rest of the town. If you guys are tired of eating MREs we can bring back some of this canned food. That is, if that's ok with you, Charlie," said Lucas.

"It's fine with me. You said you were keeping me, so my stash is your stash. Truthfully the MREs have been a great change," I replied.

"Yes, we're keeping you," said Pyka, wrapping her arms around me. I hugged her back and smiled sweetly at Lucas.

"I second that," said Dimitri, throwing a can of apple pie filling into the duffle bag.

"You were staying whether you showed us your stash or not," said Lucas with a pointed look.

We put all the panels back and headed outside.

Our silence returned as we crossed the square. The hardware store would be the next useful place to show them. Not a single lock remained on any building, but the hardware store still had a doorknob at least.

"I tried to hide at least two of everything," I said as I started pulling wall panels free.

"These aisles seem really wide," said Pyka, looking back and forth between two shelves.

"You have a good eye. I busted apart a third of the shelving in here and encased the sides of every remaining set. The shelves that face each other have tools inside." I started to pry at the center of one set and Lucas stepped in to take over. "I can do this by myself," I snapped.

He laid a heavy hand on my shoulder. Looking into my eyes and down into my very soul, he said, "You already did it once. Consider it a thank you for sharing it with us." He'd completely disarmed me. I took a deep breath and stepped back. He and Dimitri pulled apart all the shelves, surveying their contents.

The only thing Lucas chose to take was a gray rectangular, ax-grinding stone. We were halfway finished making the hardware store look empty again when I heard the rumble of the slave trucks.

"Fuck! Fuck! Fuck! We gotta hurry!" I yelled, moving faster with the wall panels.

"What do you hear?" asked Pyka, in a panic.

"The slave trucks! They're close!" I yelled.

It took another three seconds before Lucas and

Dimitri picked up on the sound. They slammed shelves together making the tools inside clatter.

"They don't typically circle the buildings," I said, heading for the door.

"I'm sure they don't typically lose a man hunting for people either," replied Lucas.

They followed me to the back of the building. We all stayed flat against the wall, hopefully out of sight from the windows. The rumble of the slave trucks shook the ground. My heart pounded as the noise got closer. The sound seemed louder as they went through the square.

Fear must have flashed across my face when I looked up at Lucas.

"What's wrong?" he asked.

I waited another moment listening before I answered him, "They aren't stopping in the square, and there are more than three trucks."

"They're headed for the camp," said Lucas.

"You said they can't get past the perimeter, right?" I asked.

"It would short circuit everything in their truck if they tried to drive through it, including the soldiers inside. You can get us close to the camp without us being seen, right?" asked Lucas.

"Follow me," I said, motioning to him and the others.

The sun was still high in the sky. We took the covered tree path I had taken the first night they saw me. They stood where I stood the night I tried to sneak past the camp. I didn't want a repeat of that adrenaline rush.

Bushes were only husks of what they used to be. Though most of the trees were dead, they somehow held some of their leaves. Between the sparce shade and the thick trunks, we couldn't be seen at this distance.

Soldiers facing outward, surrounded the perimeter of the camp. In the center of each group was a slave truck, still running. An extra slave truck faced the town, making a total of five.

"How many are there?" asked Pyka, peaking from behind a tree a bit further back from the treeline.

"At least twenty, maybe more," replied Lucas over his shoulder.

"Look at the ground between the trucks facing town," said Dimitri.

I squinted, trying to figure out what he was looking at. Boots. "Lucas, is that soldier dead?"

"Yep, poor bastard probably touched the perimeter. I doubt an elephant could survive it, a human doesn't stand a chance," replied Lucas.

"Any ideas on what to do, boss? They outnumber and out-gun us," said Dimitri.

Before Lucas could respond my brain came up with a plan. "We spread out around this big arc. One of us can fire to draw them in one direction. Once they start moving and get at least halfway across the space, another one of us shoots. Hopefully after a third shot from a different direction, they'll all be moving. If we can draw them close enough to the tree-lines, the last one still hidden can run for camp and get the big plasma gun."

"But these guns won't reach the camp from the tree line," replied Pyka.

"They don't have to. It's just to get their attention," replied Lucas. He glanced around the open, desolate space with a pensive look on his face. He stroked his beard, which I hadn't seen him do before.

"So, is that the plan, boss?" asked Dimitri.

"I don't like splitting up but it's our only option if we don't want to wait them out. Dimitri, you stay here," said Lucas, handing him the control box for the perimeter. "Charlie, show me and Pyka where we can hide further around this cul-de-sac and where we can go for cover. I'll shoot first. Once they are headed my way, you fire off a shot closer to your camp so you can hide easily. Hopefully that will distract most of them. Pyka, you fire last. Dimitri, once they're all distracted, you get your lanky ass moving. Once you clear that perimeter, I don't care how far into the tree line those damn soldiers are, you put that perimeter back up until the you're ready to fire the plasma gun."

"Yes, sir," said Dimitri, with a quick nod.

"I love you, baby," said Pyka, running up to Dimitri. It was a quick but passionate kiss.

"I love you too, baby. Go kick some ass," replied Dimitri, swatting her on her backside as she turned toward us.

CHAPTER 6

It was early afternoon when we were all settled in our spots. Lucas had no way of knowing when I was in position since we couldn't signal each other. I gave him an approximate time and he waited an extra twenty minutes before he fired his shot. The four soldiers and the truck took off toward the flash. The adrenalin surge was almost too much to handle. I had to sit and wait until they were halfway to Lucas from the camp. It was the longest distance of them all.

I made sure I was in a large tree shadow when I fired the first shot. Four soldiers and a truck headed my way. *Fuck!* Now I had to play the worst game of hide and seek in my life. I looked towards Pyka's direction. There was the flash but only one section of soldiers and a truck rolled out. *Dammit!* I ran about twenty yards and fired again. Back another ten or so yards and fired again. There, that got the rest of them moving! I looked up to see another flash from Lucas's position. The soldiers were almost to the treeline. Too damn close. I ran for the divot in the ground that sat right behind a fat tree, my biggest chance that no soldier would step on the frame that held up the dead leaves and branches. I tried to control my breathing. The heat from the day and the fear of the whole fucking situation were not helping.

Several sets of boots pounding over dead leaves made me hold my breath.

"Spread out! There's at least three of them and I want them all," barked one of the soldiers.

The sound of boots ran past me. I almost shit myself. I could hear at least one pair of boots heading towards my sanctuary. *Fuck*! Guess I'll be moving again.

"Someone's living out here," a different voice yelled.

BOOM! BOOM! The two explosions didn't sound the same. Dimitri must have hit a truck. The thunderous noise didn't make my ears ring this time, since I was in a hole. Noted. Boots clomped by me at a run. *BOOM! BOOM!* Yes! Another truck gone! *BOOM! BOOM!* Those two explosions were followed by accelerating engines and then silence.

I waited another ten minutes before venturing out of my hole. I kept a tight grip on the plasma gun trying to remember how many shots I had left. I took slow steps to stay quiet, but it was futile. Thankfully my part of the forest was empty.

The site that surrounded the camp was surreal. Three trucks lay on their sides, sending black smoke into the sky. Bodies surrounded two of the trucks. I glanced around the once completely open space and saw no movement. *Fuck!* I hope Lucas and Pyka were still alive.

Something caught my eye. Dimitri stepped from the other side of our truck. He was waving his arms. Lucas stepped out into the open next. I finally let out the breath I'd been holding. I started making my way toward the camp when Pyka cleared her treeline. We did it! We all made it.

CHAPTER 7

After a shower, I climbed on top of our truck. Sitting on the opposite side from our camp, I let one leg hang, my right elbow resting on my bent knee. The generator was the only thing I could hear. Not that much of anything made noise out here, unless the wind blew, or it rained. At least the weather still worked normally. Even birds were a rarity, at that, they were scavenger birds. What I wouldn't give to see birds with some color. The stench of burnt oil still lingered in the air as I looked around. The bodies of the slave trader soldiers were gone, but their incapacitated trucks remained. I always tried to see the beauty in the wasteland, but now, that beauty was tainted. Sure, we could disassemble the trucks and drag them off to … I don't know where. A junk yard, I guess. But the spilled chemicals would leave dark stains on the earth, a constant reminder of death, of the enemy we had to fight, of the fear we lived in outside of the perimeter. Thankfully the black stain of the soldier who touched the perimeter at the same time Dimitri pulled the trigger on his plasma gun wasn't person shaped. But, it too added to my sorrow. I took a deep breath and tried to focus on the trees that covered the rolling hills surrounding my oasis.

As the events of the last two days replayed in my head, the closing of the truck door shook me from my thoughts.

"Where's Charlie?" I heard Lucas ask, but only because my ears were apparently already attuned to his voice. I didn't hear a reply to his question but seconds later I heard his boots as he ascended the ladder.

"Hi Lucas," I said, turning my head to look up at him. I didn't recognize my own voice. It was a little more than a whisper.

"What's going on inside that beautiful head?" Lucas asked, sitting behind me further back on the truck. His thick, strong hands gripped my hips. It sent tingles in every direction. He dragged me effortlessly back into the V of his outstretched legs.

I leaned back against his hard chest. He wrapped his left arm around my shoulders, which I gripped with both hands. When his right arm wrapped around my waist, I felt locked in and safe. I breathed a heavy sigh of relief before more emotions bubbled up and stung my eyes. "Do you want the truth?"

"Always," he replied in a low and soothing tone.

"I'm torn. You, Pyka, and Dimitri drew the attention of the slave traders to my hidden sanctuary. My invisibility is gone. That was my defense. The other side of this coin is that you have the power to defend yourselves *and* me against the slave traders, evidenced by the surrounding carnage," I said, looking around again. "Having friends and the best night's sleep I'd had in years is priceless after being alone so long."

"This is a lot of change in a short period of time. You're still processing." The way his voice rumbled through me helped to still my thoughts.

"Are you a psychologist or a medical doctor?" I asked teasingly.

"My roommate in college was a psych major," said Lucas with a short laugh. "He learned to see through all of our bullshit. We even made a game out of it. I learned a lot that year.

We were silent for a few moments. Tingles rippled over my skin where Lucas' fingertips rubbed in slow, lazy circles. It still felt new, yet seemed like it had always been. I stared at the spot in the tree line where I usually entered. The bare spot told me I needed to change it up if I ever went back to my hiding spot in the trees.

"Your quick thinking saved us today," Lucas said, startling me, making me jump. "Sorry."

"How so?" I asked.

"Making it look like several people were shooting from your area. You waited far longer than I liked before going to hide, but it saved us." I detected a streak of protectiveness in his tone along with the gratitude.

"That's something I don't get. When I'm alone I feel like I have... well not balls of steel. But I can think, I can move quickly, I can survive. When this happens," I said, tapping on the arm I was still clinging to. "I feel vulnerable but safe. I know we're on top of this truck, exposed, and probably out of range of the electric perimeter, but I still feel like nothing can touch me wrapped in your arms. I've known you all of what? Two days? Three? What is this? And where the hell did my nerve go? And is this something you want?" I asked. That last thought suddenly put fear in my heart.

"You *are* safe," said Lucas tightening his arms just a bit. "And yes, I want you here. Not to mention Pyka would kill me if I let you go back into the forest alone. Dimitri's happy to have you here too. He's already pried open that can of apple filling." I smiled at what he said. "Relationships are more important to all of us since the risk of losing your life is much higher."

"Or at least your freedom," I replied. "Seeing those people in those slave trucks the other day was heart wrenching."

"We need to see how big the slave traders' base is. If we knock it out of commission, maybe we can have some peace for a while," said Lucas.

"The thought of peace, if only temporary, strongly conflicts with the immeasurable risk of going near the traders' base."

"It's inevitable. Only two trucks left here today. Dimitri and I buried eighteen bodies."

"So, we're taking the fight to them?" I asked, already knowing the answer.

"We'll scout tomorrow and come up with a

plan."

The gravity of the situation hit me. We were about to climb into a den of venomous snakes. *Shit!*

Lucas and Dimitri spent the rest of the evening in the third, uninhabited tent. Pyka and I weren't allowed in it. Apparently, Pyka had never even been inside of it. Lucas explained that it was extra supplies and the equipment to recharge all the plasma guns. If we were ever captured, Pyka and I couldn't be tortured into showing the slave traders how to use it.

While the guys were preparing for tomorrow, Pyka and I went to my former dwelling to grab a few things. It was nice to have a real friend to talk to. It seemed like I wouldn't speak for days when I was on my own. The only time I really talked out loud was cursing while hiding from the slave traders.

On the way, I showed her some of the covered divots in the ground where I had hidden from them. Once inside my covered cave, I explained how my water filtration system worked. As she studied the workings of the charcoal filters, I grabbed what I felt would be of use for tomorrow. She helped me carry a couple of jugs of water to replenish the reservoir in the truck.

It was after dark when I heard Lucas and Dimitri's voices. They must be finished preparing for tomorrow. It startled me when Lucas jerked the entrance fabric of our tent open. "I'm surprised you're still awake. I'm going to go shower," he said. "I just wanted to let you know we were finished."

It was hard to keep my eyes open until Lucas returned. We slipped into the same position he had given me instructions for the previous night. The spicy smell of his soap invaded my senses, helping me relax even more. Locked in his embrace, I crashed. Hard. Again.

CHAPTER 8

Morning slammed into me like a wrecking ball. I inhaled Lucas's scent trying to stave off the day for a few more seconds. Looking up, his eyes saw right through me.

"You gonna be okay?" he asked.

"Losing you and the others is not on my list of things I'd like to do today," I replied, pushing myself out of bed.

"It's not on mine either, but if we need to fight today, we need to do it like we're all coming out of this alive and free."

It felt good being strapped into my harness. I knew we'd be fighting soldiers with plasma guns, but the machetes strapped to my back gave me the feeling of extra security. On one leg was a holster with a plasma pistol. We each had at least two plasma guns hidden out of sight.

Once we exited the perimeter we headed to my area of the forest. I showed Lucas one of the more hidden divots to put the control box for the perimeter in. The truck was too important to lose.

The sun was bright. The breeze felt good against my face as we traversed the empty, rocky space towards town. I was thankful to be upwind of the trucks. "I know we just ate but let's stop by the grocery store. Think I have some dried fruit stashed so we don't get hungry on this little scouting expedition."

Lucas arched an eyebrow at me. "You're stalling."

"You're right, but it's a probably a long walk to the traders' base." I countered, with a smirk.

Pyka laughed at our exchange. Siding with me, she said, "I want some snacks too." She threw Dimitri an innocent look.

"We can't outvote her now, Lucas," Dimitri chuckled.

"We're bigger, of course we can," replied Lucas, giving me a wicked smirk of his own.

I swung open the grocery store door like I always do. Lucas, Dimitri, and Pyka stayed outside looking at the slave traders' truck tracks. They wanted to get a bead on the right direction to go. Just as I reached the back of the store, I heard yelling and a plasma gun blast. *Fuck!* I spun around to head back out but came face to face with the barrel of another plasma gun. *Double fuck!*

"If our captain didn't want you alive, I'd end your life right now," the soldier snarled. "Take off your harness!"

Dammit! There goes the extra protection. I slowly moved to unlatch the harness from my belt. The moment I thought about reaching for my plasma gun, the soldier removed it from my leg holster. *Shit!*

"Put your hands on your head." I followed his orders, feeling more exposed than ever. "Move!" He motioned his pistol towards the door.

I heard a slave truck roar to life behind another one of the stores in the square. How had I not heard it? Did it come back during the night or is it one of the trucks that fled yesterday? If that's the case, all of these soldiers saw eighteen of their comrades die. Couple that with the fact that they probably didn't sleep. These men were on a razor's edge. One fuck up and we were all dead despite their captain's orders.

I never wanted to be on this side of the cage. Contrary to their usual practice, one of the soldiers stayed in the back with us. We were put in each corner so we couldn't talk. *Fuck!*

I had never sought out the slave traders' base camp, nor had I come across it in my explorations. When we pulled up to a gated facility more than a day's walk from my town, I was surprised to see a jail. Not quite a small county jail, but not a federal prison either. I really hoped that we wouldn't be put in a cell with other criminals. Studying the soldier's face more closely gave me a clue. The very telling tattoo on the side of his face reminded me that the criminals were now the jailers. *Fuck!*

Our hands on our heads, we were marched deep into the jail. Once again, I had resolved myself to death. I reveled in the momentary increase in company but didn't expect that to extend past today.

They marched us down a corridor. I longed to

put my hands over my nose. The stench of dried sweat nauseated me.

"Put them in separate cells," one of them bellowed. "The captain will deal with them once the slaves are in for lunch."

"Yes, sir," another soldier answered, unlocking the cell in front of me.

Well fuck! We were all the way in this, and Lucas was out of my line of sight. Time to be a distraction. "You shitheads aren't going to get away with this!" I shouted. My only hope was that Lucas, Dimitri, and Pyka could somehow make it out of this mess alive...eventually. The soldier slapped me across the face, making my head snap. For a few seconds, I saw stars. Once my vision cleared, I reared my foot back and kicked him in the shin with my hard boot. He roared before grabbing me by the throat. He slammed me against the brick wall and yelled, "Do you wanna die now?" His breath washed over my face. Minty fresh. He had access to toothpaste. Something to relieve the slave traders of along with any other supplies they had stashed. I stayed silent, trying to form a plan.

"Search her and the others before you lock them up," said the first soldier. He shoved me in the cell and kicked my feet apart. I reached back to grab my braid to hold it out of his way. The soldier ran his hands down my legs, finding two more plasma pistols. He found nothing as he ran his hands along my outstretched arms. I breathed a sigh of relief when they slid the cell door closed and locked it.

They hadn't touched my hair. In that moment, I had renewed hope that I could get us out...or get us killed trying. Either way, we would never be slaves.

I listened as Lucas, Dimitri, and Pyka were put into cells. It was one long corridor so I couldn't see them. It seemed like we were at least two cells apart. That meant we couldn't see or communicate with each other to make a plan.

Lucas waited until all was quiet before he checked in on us. "Charlie, are you okay?"

"I could use some ice but other than that, I'm good." I replied. I could feel the left side of my face swelling. The sting was still very much present.

"Pyka and Dimitri, are you two okay?" Lucas continued.

"I'm good," said Pyka. Her voice no longer held a jovial tone.

"Pissed, but good," replied Dimitri. "How about you?"

"Livid, but physically okay," replied Lucas.

We all went quiet after that. Time to plan by myself. I sat on the edge of one of the beds. No soldiers were in my direct line of sight. Perfect! I had some privacy, so I unbraided my hair.

What finally fell loose when I reached the top was akin to a two-foot chain with a leather wrapped handle. Welded off of each link was a metal barb, bent downwards.

Pyka hadn't seen me put it in my leg pouch yesterday. I had done my hair after Lucas left the tent to start the fire for breakfast. I didn't know if I'd actually have the opportunity to use it, so I kept it a secret. I also didn't want to show it off and get cocky. That's not what we needed today.

My fingers were sore by the time I had straightened all the barbs. Even more so when I worked hard enough to snap two of the barbs off closest to the handle.

I listened hard for any movement. I went to each end of my cell to see as far down the corridor as possible. There were no soldiers that I could see. My heart pounded as I reached through the bars on each side of the lock. Using the two-inch barbs, I began picking the lock. I estimated at least fifteen minutes had passed when the lock disengaged. Relief flooded me, followed by *now what?* That question was answered when I heard at least two sets of boot laden footsteps coming down the corridor. I stepped back, leaning my shoulder against the wall. My makeshift weapon dangled from my hand behind me.

The soldier pulled out his keys to unlock my door. When he grabbed one of the bars, the door moved. He looked at the lock in confusion as the door slid open. I took the chance and swung. The barbed chain slashed him across the face. He hollered and stumbled back, knocking into the soldier behind him, making him drop his plasma gun. I scrambled for it. Turning around, I fired at least four shots. I hated death, but I loved my friends more.

Adrenaline rushed through me, making my

hands shake. I holstered the gun and grabbed the keys, unlocking Pyka's cell door first.

"Thank you, Charlie," she said, with gratefulness in her voice.

"You're welcome. Now go grab the plasma gun." I replied, pointing at the two men in a heap. I was sure someone had heard the sounds of the altercation.

Pyka ran to the dead soldiers and grabbed the other plasma gun. Another soldier started down the corridor from the opposite direction. Pyka fired past me as I was unlocking Lucas' door. I tossed him the keys to let Dimitri out, just in time to fire at another soldier. Pyka and I retrieved the soldiers' plasma guns, tossing them to the guys. I knew I was down at least five shots, so my aim had to be perfect.

I aimed in the direction of the footsteps but stopped short. It was the people who were enslaved coming in for lunch. Their eyes went wide as we headed in their direction. They parted for us. When I got a clear shot of the next soldier, I fired. I pulled his plasma gun from his holster and handed it to the closest person. "Lead us out of here," I commanded. With a quick nod, he immediately took off in front of me. He took out the next two soldiers and relieved them of their guns. There were more enslaved people than soldiers. Even though not all of them were armed, I'm sure it was a frightening sight to the next set of soldiers. They just pulled out their guns and fired, not bothering to aim. They killed three or four of the unarmed slaves. Those of us who had guns, fired. I hated killing people but, it was an us or them situation.

We rounded the corner, encountering the next group of soldiers. The shock gave us enough time to get shots off. Their guns got handed out and soon we had an army of overworked men and women who were way past ready to be free.

"Take us to the supply warehouse," I told the first guy, once we thought the facility was cleared.

"This way," he replied. He led us out of the jail to a separate building.

All of the enslaved people followed us. We were almost free.

The building door swung open before I could try the first key.

"Stop!" bellowed a deep, angry voice. Out stepped who must have been the captain. He was dressed only slightly nicer than the other soldiers. Though he was outnumbered, the plasma gun in his hand rivaled the one sitting in our tent. We all froze. That cannon would take out most, if not all of us, in one shot. "Get back to your cells! Your rations just got cut in half! And for every one of my soldiers that's dead, I'm going to cut out one of your eyes with a rusty spoon!" *So. Fucking. Close.*

I saw movement out of the corner of my eye, followed by the sound of a blast. Down went the captain. He dropped the plasma gun and we all jumped out of the way, fearing it would go off. We stood in silence for a few moments.

"Bastard had it commin'," snarled this tiny

woman in her fifties who didn't clear the five-foot mark. She had more lines on her face than a city map. Her hands looked like tanned leather. Both were evidence of the hard life she must have lived. She walked towards him with her plasma gun still pointed at him, then looked up at me. "We were plannin' on doing this ourselves, we just hadn't figured out how to get going. Guess you beat us to it. Much appreciated."

I nodded. "Was it enough to take a share of these supplies?"

"Everybody gets a share, slaves or not. Life is too damn tough. Now let's get this split up and get the hell out of here," she replied.

"Yes, ma'am," I said, moving towards the warehouse.

I opened the metal door and peeked in. "I think it's clear." I said before entering. Lucas grabbed my arm before I could set one foot inside.

"Let us go first," he said. He and Dimitri disappeared into the darkness since it was so bright outside. A few moments later, the big bay doors started to retract.

The next few hours were spent dividing the supplies. The slave trucks were used to haul loads to a few surrounding towns. They were determined to rebuild. The people who were enslaved were forced to dig for long hours looking for signs of plant and animal life. Even the criminals were smart enough to know food would eventually run out, and the only real way to survive was to replenish the earth. While a brilliant idea, the people wanted to do it on their own terms.

It was almost dark when we climbed up into a slave truck to head home. It was surreal to ride in one after hiding from them for so long, albeit in the cab. And when we made it to our camp, I could exit of my volition. We were free.

Though we kept a few things, a lot of our supplies got hidden in stores...just in case. Tomorrow we would increase the size of the perimeter. The slave truck could sit outside of it for one night.

It had been an emotional and exhausting day. We all wanted a shower and some sleep. The guys got the fire going while Pyka and I took turns showering. Even on the second day, the shower felt amazing. I wondered if that would ever change. Lucas was the last to shower. Instead of sitting in his own chair after he stepped out of the truck, he walked over and picked me up out of mine. I was thankful it was a sturdy wooden chair when he sat down and plopped me in his lap. I couldn't quite read the look on his face.

"What is it, Lucas?" I asked, my heart suddenly pounding. I knew I was sitting in his lap, but was he about to send me packing?

"Life's a bitch sometimes and sometimes that life gets cut short. I know you're staying with us, but uh, how about making my tent your permanent residence?" His face poured sweat. I could see his pulse racing through the vein in his neck.

"Yes," I barely had time to reply when he sealed my answer with a searing kiss. *Fuck yes!* I was wanted! I was cared for! I was...loved? Maybe not yet, but I'm sure it would come soon. Lucas' kiss stole my breath. "You're mine," he growled after breaking the kiss.

Dimitri, not to be out done, practically set Pyka's face on fire with a scorching kiss of his own. "You're still mine," he said when he let her go.

"Forever, baby," Pyka giggled, and then kissed him back with just a much fire.

Later that night, I could hardly keep my eyes open as I stroked Lucas' beard. "So, you don't just want me because I can kick some ass?" I asked playfully.

"No, not just because you can kick some ass," Lucas replied.

He kissed my forehead and then locked me in place. We crashed. Hard.

The end!!!

ABOUT THE AUTHOR

Amaya Sego

Thank you so much for reading this short story! I know it was a quick read but it was fun to write. This was my first post-apocalyptic short story, so please leave a few words and some stars. I would greatly appreciate it. This is the second work that I've published after Inventions Airships and Armored Corsets which can also be found on KU.

My other passion is costuming. While writing this short story, I dabbled in dystopian costuming. You can see this along with my steampunk costumes on my social media accounts. TikTok: @amayasego Instagram:@amayasego

www.ingramcontent.com/pod-product-compliance
Lightning Source LLC
Chambersburg PA
CBHW020319150626
46552CB00022B/2982